"It brings back memories of my Yuki-Little Lake grandmother, whose gentle hands raised me."

— **Darlene Brown Toyebo**, Concow, Yuki-Little Lake and Shoshone-Bannock Indian

"*Cheewa James has caught the flavor of the Native American thought and spirit.*"

— **Billy Mills,** Sioux, 1964 Olympic gold-medalist

"*The writings and the music accompanying the book recall a heritage as rich and old as our Mother Earth.*"

— *Joan Ainslie,* Mohawk and Tuscarora

"*Understanding the beauty of another culture is powerful.*"

— *Les Brown,* motivational speaker

"*The music is absolutely breathtaking. It has lingered with me for days.*"

— *Bill Follis,* chief, Modoc Tribe of Oklahoma

Cover design: Cheewa James/Annegra Hart
Page design and layout: Annegra Hart
Clyde "Chief" James photo: Peter Haley
Back cover photo: Ben Newbold

Catch the Whisper of the Wind

CLYDE "CHIEF" JAMES
Modoc, 1900-1982

by Cheewa James

Published by HORIZON 2000
3330 Union Springs Way
Sacramento, CA 95827
First Edition

Library of Congress Catalog Number 92-090230

ISBN number   0-9632665-0-0

This book is dedicated to my father

Clyde "Chief" James
1900-1982

and

my two sons

David J. and Todd Easterla

The three men who have most profoundly
touched my life....

Acknowledgements

Catch the Whisper of the Wind is a vision quest.

The vision is one that calls upon all people to feel the heartbeat of humanity, acknowledging the wealth and excitement of human diversity.

The quest of searching out another people's spirit and philosophy is a compelling one. Each culture offers knowledge, insight and joy.

Catch the Whisper of the Wind has been a spiritual adventure that has made friends of strangers and soulmates of friends. It has reinforced the thought that a worthy vision quest is an attraction for the positive thinkers and the givers of the world.

This is a humble undertaking. It is only a small glimpse of the sensitivity of American Indian thinking and culture. To the vision seeker, so much remains to be unveiled and pondered.

The richness of Native American culture awaits those who explore the message of this book and the accompanying narration and music.

I acknowledge the dedication, spirit and love that Annegra Hart has given to this project. She has done page layout, tapped resources and spent late night hours critiquing the music and words George and I wove.

Composer/musician George Tricomi was a delightful companion as we explored together the aura of American Indian music — and took the traditional and combined it with innovative, new compositions. He called on the sounds of many worlds and cultures to weave into his music.

What a joy it was to find Jean Villaseñor and feel the connection with her lovely spirit. In her words, "The spiritual foundation of this continent has already been laid by the American Indian."

I extend my appreciation to Naturegraph Publishers, Inc., located in Happy Camp, California, for granting permission to use the Villaseñor's works from *Indian Designs*.

Thanks to Bud Gardner for the warmth and caring of his friendship and for the support that he so willingly extended.

To my friend, photographer Peter Haley, I am grateful for the mystical picture of my father, Clyde "Chief" James, taken before my father rounded the arc in the circle of life.

Raymond Haring, with all his computer knowledge, was so helpful, particularly with the transferring of the illustrations. He, too, came under their spell.

I would like to acknowledge Darlene Brown Toyebo's friendship and encouragement. She is a special friend. My thanks also to Joan Ainslie and Paulette Kelley for their contribution of Native American quotes.

Cheewa James

Forward

The Native American voice was once a mighty roar across this land.

But just as the vast buffalo herds once thundered across the plains and are no more, the voice of the American Indian has faded to a whisper.

The powerful voice and the age-old wisdom of the Native American — carried in drumbeat and passed from tongue to tongue as the evening fires met the twilight — still live.

The timeless philosophy and principles for living await those who choose to

— Catch the Whisper of the Wind —

What

Is

Life?

What is life?

It is the flash of a firefly
in the night.

It is the breath of a buffalo
in the winter time.

It is the little shadow
which runs across the grass
and loses itself in the Sunset.

1   *— Crowfoot, Blackfoot Indian*

My heart is filled with joy
   when I see you here,
   as the brooks fill with water
   when the snow melts
   in the spring;

And I feel glad as the ponies do
   when the fresh grass starts
   in the beginning of the year...

I was born upon the prairie
   where the wind blew free
   and there was nothing to
   break the light of the sun...

Do not ask us
   to give up the buffalo
      for the sheep.

2   — *Ten Bears, Commanche*

We are part fire, and part
dream.
We are the physical
mirroring of Miaheyyun,
the Total Universe,
upon this earth,
our Mother.

We are here to experience.
We are a movement of a hand
within millions of seasons,
a wink of touching within
millions and millions
of sun fires.

And we speak
with the mirroring of the sun.

3   — *Fire Dog, Cheyenne*

Look and listen for
the welfare of the whole people
and have always in view
not only the present
but also
the coming generations,
even those whose faces
are yet beneath
the surface of the earth—
the unborn of the future Nation.

4   —*Constitution of the Five Nations*

When legends die,
there are no more dreams.

When there are no more dreams,
there is no more greatness.

5   — *anonymous*

Everything
the Power of the World does
is done in a circle.

The sky
is round, and I have
heard that the earth is round
like a ball and so are all the stars.
The wind, in its greatest power,
whirls. Birds make their nests in
circles, for theirs is the same
religion as ours. The sun
comes forth and goes
down again in a
circle. The
moon does
the same, and
both are round. Even
the seasons form a great
circle in their changing and always come back where they were.
The life of a man is a circle from
childhood to childhood, and
so it is in everything
where power
moves.

— *Black Elk, Oglala Sioux*

Look at your
neighbor and make him sparkle.

Your eyes
are the mirror of your soul.

When you sparkle your eyes,
    whether you think
        you are beautiful or not,
        you are.

7   — *Twylah Nitsch, Seneca*

Wars are fought to see
who owns the land, but in
the end it possesses man. Who
dares say he owns it — is he
not buried beneath it?

8   — *Cochise, Chiricahua Apache*

I wish all to know
that I do not propose to sell
any part of my country,
nor
will I have the whites
cutting our timber
along the rivers,
more especially the oak.

I am particularly fond of the
little groves of oak trees.
I love to look at them,
because
they endure the wintry storm
and the summer's heat, and
— not unlike ourselves —
seem to flourish
by them.

— *Sitting Bull, Hunkpapa Sioux*

You must teach your children
    that the ground beneath
    their feet is the ashes
    of our grandfathers.

So that they will respect the land,
    tell your children that
    the earth is rich with
    the lives of our kin.

Teach your children what
    we have taught our children,
    that the earth is our mother.

Whatever befalls the Earth
    befalls the sons of the Earth.

If men spit upon the ground
    they spit upon themselves.

This we know.
    The Earth does not
    belong to man,
    man belongs to Earth.

This we know.
    All things are connected
    like the blood which
    unites one family.

All things are connected.
    Whatever befalls the Earth
    befalls the sons of the Earth.

    Man did not weave
    the web of life;
    he is merely a strand in it.

Whatever he does to the web,
    he does to himself.

— *Chief Seattle, Duwamish*

In the life of the Indian
there was only one inevitable
duty,
— the duty of prayer —
the daily recognition
of the Unseen and Eternal...
Each soul
must meet the morning sun,
the new, sweet earth, and
the Great Silence
alone.

Whenever,
in the course of the daily hunt
the red hunter comes
upon a scene
that is strikingly
beautiful or sublime

— a black thundercloud
with the rainbow's glowing arch
above the mountain,

a white waterfall
in the heart of a green gorge,

a vast prairie tinged
with the blood-red of sunset

— he pauses for an instant
in the attitude of worship.

He sees no need
for setting apart
one day in seven as a holy day,
since to him
all days are God's.

11   — *Ohiyesa, Santee Sioux*

Did you know that trees talk?
Well they do.

They talk to each other,
and
they'll talk to you
if
you listen...

I have learned a lot from trees:
sometimes
about the weather,
sometimes
about animals,
sometimes
about the Great Spirit.

— *Walking Buffalo,*
Canadian Stoney Indian

At the edge of the cornfield
a bird will sing with them
in the oneness of
their happiness.

So they will sing together in tune
with the universal power,
in harmony with
the one Creator
of all things.

And the bird song,
and the people's song,
and the song of life
will become one.

13— Song of the Long Hair Kachinas, Hopi

Kinship
with all creatures
of the earth, sky, and water
was a real and active principle...

And so close
did some of the Lakotas
come to their feathered and
furred friends that in
true brotherhood
they spoke
a common tongue.

The animals had rights —
    the right of man's protection,
    the right to live,
    the right to multiply,
    the right to freedom, and
    the right to man's indebtedness.

14   *—Luther Standing Bear, Teton Sioux*

Animals and plants are taught
by Wakan tanka
what they are to do.

Wakan tanka
teaches the birds to make nests,
yet the nests of all birds
are not alike.

Wakan tanka
gives them merely the outline.
Some make better nests
than others...

The reason Wakan tanka
does not make two birds,
or animals,
or human beings exactly alike
is because each is placed here by
Wakan tanka
to be an independent
individuality and to rely on itself...

It is the same with
human beings;
there is some place which
is best adapted to each...

All living creatures and all plants
are a benefit to something...

A man ought to
desire that which is genuine
instead of that which is
artificial.

Long ago there was no such
thing as a mixture of earths
to make paint.

There were only three colors
of native earth paint
— red, white and black.
These could be obtained
only in certain places.

When other colors were desired,
the Indians mixed the
juices of plants,
but it was found
that these mixed colors faded
and it could always be told
when the red was genuine
— the red made of burned clay.

— *Okute, Teton Sioux*

The Lakota thought of air
much the same way
as the white man
does of water —
something cleansing,
something to bathe in.

Our bodies bathed in air, and
breathing was not only
conducted through nose
and lungs but with
the entire body...

Bodies were nourished
not only by food...
wind, rain and sun
also nourished.

16   *— Luther Standing Bear, Lakota*

A Nation is not conquered
until the hearts of its women
are on the ground.

Then it is done,
no matter how brave its
warriors
nor how strong its weapons.

17   *— Traditional Cheyenne saying*

When you get married
do not make an idol
of the woman you marry;
do not worship her.

If you worship a woman
she will insist upon
greater and greater
worship as time goes on.

18   — *Sam Blow Snake, Winnebago*

It is not only now
that woman causes trouble.

That has been
since first man was.

19   — *Father of Thunderchild, Plains Cree*

Marriage
among my people
was like traveling in a canoe.

The man
sat in front
and paddled the canoe.

The woman
sat in the stern but
she steered.

20   — *anonymous*

I never did get a woman
　　that thought the way I did.

It's like a guessing game.

**If you don't
　　know anything about it,
　　　　you guess wrong
　　　　　　and lose.**

　　　　　　　　　　　　— *Navajo man*

It is well
to be good to women
in the strength of our manhood
because
we must sit under their hands
at both ends of our lives.

22   — *He Dog, Oglala Sioux*

Love songs
are dangerous.

If a man gets to singing them
we send for a medicine man
to treat him and
make him
stop.

23   — *anonymous, Papago*

A man
was chief only as long
as he did the will of the people.

If he got
to be too chiefy,
he'd go to sleep one night,
and wake up the next morning
to find that he was chief
all to himself.

The tribe would
move away in the night,
and they didn't wait four years
to do it, either.

24   — *Sun Bear, Chippewa*

Training began with children
who were taught to sit still
and enjoy it.

They were taught
to use their organs of smell,
to look when there was
apparently nothing to see,
and to listen
intently when all seemingly
was quiet.

A child that cannot sit still is a
half-developed child.

25   *— Luther Standing Bear, Lakota*

If you do bad things
  your children will follow you
   and do the same.

If you want to raise
  good children,
    be decent yourself.

26   *— In-the-Middle, Mescalero Apache*

Good acts
done for the love
of children become
stories good for the ears
of people from other bands.

They become as coveted things,
and are placed side by side
with the stories of war
achievements.

27   *— Social tradition, Assiniboine*

Do not speak of evil
      for it creates curiosity in
            the minds of the young.

28   — *Lakota proverb*

Lose your temper with a child
and you will age in sorrow.

29   — *Algonquin proverb*

Children
   must early learn the
      beauty of generosity.

They are taught to give what
   they prize most,
      that they may taste the
         happiness of giving.

The Indians in their simplicity
   literally give away
      all that they have —

   to relatives,
   to guests of other tribes
   or clans,
   but above all
   to the poor and
   the aged,

   from whom they can
   hope for no return.

—Ohiyesa, Santee Sioux

My young men
shall never work.
Men who work cannot dream;
and wisdom comes to us
in dreams.

You ask me to plow the ground.
Shall I take a knife and
tear my mother's breast?
Then when I die
she will not
take me
to her bosom
to rest.

You ask me to dig for stone.
Shall I dig under her skin
for her bones?

Then when I die I cannot
enter her body to be born again.

You ask me to cut grass and
make hay and
sell it and
be rich
like white men.
But how dare I cut off my
mother's hair?

31   — *Smohalla, Nez Perce*

The
man who
sat on the
ground in his tipi
meditating on life and
its meaning, accepting the
kinship of all creatures and
acknowledging unity with the
universe of things　was infusing
into his being the▲true essence
of civilization.

32　　　　　　　*— Luther Standing Bear, Lakota*

We who are clay
blended by the Master Potter,
come from the kiln of Creation
in many hues.

How can people say one skin is
colored, when each has its own
coloration?

What should it matter
that one bowl is dark
and the other pale,
if each is
of good design
and serves its purpose well.

33   — *Polingaysi Qoyawayma, Hopi*

He who is present at a
wrongdoing
and lifts not a hand
to prevent it,
is as guilty
as the wrongdoers.

34   — *Estamaza, Omaha*

Even if
the heavens
were to fall on me,
I want to do what is right...
I never do wrong
without a cause.

35   — *Geronimo, Chiricahua Apache*

Let me be a free man —
    free to travel,
    free to stop,
    free to work,
    free to trade where I choose,
    free to choose
        my own teachers,
    free to follow the
        religion of my fathers,
    free to talk and think
    and act for myself —

and I will obey every law
or submit to the penalty.

36   *— Chief Joseph, Nez Perce*

The Yani Indian Ishi, America's last stoneage Indian, stepped out of his pre-history world in 1911 to be confronted with a startling, exciting, bewildering new world.

On his death, five years later, his friend Dr. Saxton Pope said:

**"He looked upon us
as sophisticated children
— smart,
but not wise.**

**We knew many things,
and much that is false.**

**He knew nature,
which is always true.**

His were the qualities of
character that last forever.

He was kind;
he had courage and self-
restraint,

and though all
had been taken from him,
there was no bitterness
in his heart.

His soul
was that of a child,
his mind that of a philosopher."

37   *— Dr. Saxton Pope*

Every struggle,
whether won or lost,
strengthens us for the
next to come.

It is not good for people
to have an easy life.
They become
weak and inefficient
when they cease to struggle.

Some need
a series of defeats before
developing the strength and
courage to win a victory.

38   *— Victorio, Mimbres Apache*

I will not lie to you.
I do not deceive you.
I come to lead.

39   *— Cochise, Chiricahua Apache*

Just what Power is
   I cannot explain,
      for it is beyond
         my comprehension.

Those who seek it
   go alone that
      they may be tested
         for worthiness.

It is a gift
   to be bestowed
      not only for virtue but
         for prayer and
            courage.

— *Victorio, Mimbres Apache*

In you,
as in all men,
are natural powers.

You have a will.
Learn to use it.
Make it work for you.

Sharpen your senses
as you sharpen your knife...

We can give you nothing.
You already possess everything
necessary to become great.

41   — *Legendary Dwarf Chief, Crow*

When you begin a great work
you can't expect to finish it
all at once; therefore,
you and your
brothers
press on,
and let nothing discourage you
till you have entirely finished
what you have begun...

Though you may hear birds
singing on this side and
that side, you must
not take notice
of that,
but hear me
when I speak to you,
and take it to heart, for you
may always depend
that what I say
shall be true.

42   — *Teedyuscung, Delaware*

You must speak straight
so that your words may go
as sunlight into
our hearts.

43   —*Cochise, Chiricahua Apache*

As a man is
climbing up he
does something
that marks a place
in his life where the
powers have given him
the opportunity to express
in acts his peculiar endowments,

so this
place, this act,
forms a stage in
his career, and he
takes a new name to
indicate that he is on a
level different from that
which he occupied previously.
Some men can rise only a little
way, others live on a dead level.

Men having power to advance,
climb step by step.

44 — The Kurahus Tahirussawichi, Pawnee

The Indian believes
profoundly in silence —
the sign of a perfect
equilibrium.

Silence is the
absolute poise or
balance of body,
mind and spirit.

The man who preserves
his selfhood is ever calm
and unshaken by the
storms of existence...

What are the fruits of silence?
They are self-control,
true courage or
endurance, patience,
dignity, and reverence.

Silence is the
cornerstone of character.

— *Ohiyesa, Santee Sioux*

Peace...
comes within the souls of men
when they realize their
relationship, their oneness,
with the universe

and
all its powers,

and
when they realize that
at the center of the Universe
dwells Wankan tanka,

and
that this center
is really everywhere.
It is
within each of us.

46   — *Black Elk, Oglala Sioux*

Have patience.
　　All things change
　　　　in due time.

Wishing cannot
　　bring autumn glory or
　　　　cause winter to cease.

47　　　　　　　　　— *Ginaly-li, Cherokee*

The longer a problem
　　is allowed to exist,
　　　　the harder it is to
　　　　　　return to peace of mind.

48　　　　　　　　— *Twylah Nitsch, Seneca*

The selfish man is lonely, and
his untended fire dies.

49   — *Pima man*

Free yourself
from negative influence.
Negative thoughts are the old
habits that gnaw at the roots
of the soul.

50   — *Moses Shongo, Seneca*

A brave man dies but once —
cowards are always dying.

51   — *Moanahonga, Iowa*

One has to face fear
or forever run from it.

52   — *Hawk, Crow*

Do not judge
your neighbor until
you walk two moons in
his moccasins.

53   — *Northern Cheyenne proverb*

Kindness
is to use one's will
to guard one's speech and
conduct so as not to injure
anyone.

54   — *Omaha oral tradition*

Lose your temper
and you lose a friend;

Lie and you lose yourself.

55   *— Hopi proverb*

To be lazy
   while there is plenty
      means death
         when there is little.

56   *— Winnebago proverb*

Do not stop watering the corn
while you count on
the clouds to
bring rain.

57   — *Dan George*

The Ute who follows two rabbits
will perhaps catch one,
and often none.

58   — *Dan George*

Honor age!
Even an old blind man
may guide you to
a rainbow.

59   — *Micmac proverb*

No one likes to be criticized,
but criticism
can be something
like the desert wind that,
in whipping the tender corn
stalks, forces them to strike
their roots down deeper for
security.

60   — *Polingaysi Qoyawayma, Hopi*

My father sent for me.

I saw he was dying.
I took his hand in mine...
He said: "Always remember
that your father
never sold his country...

Never forget my dying words.
This country holds your
father's body.

Never sell the bones of your
father and your mother..."

I buried him in that beautiful
valley of winding waters.
I love that land more than
all the rest of the world.

A man who would
not love his father's grave
is worse than a wild animal.

— *Chief Joseph, Nez Perce*

We live, we die,
and,
like the grass and trees,
renew ourselves
from the soft clods of the grave.

Stones crumble and decay,
faiths grow old
and they are forgotten,
but new beliefs are born.

The faith of the villages
is dust now,
but
it will grow
again like the trees.

62   — *Old One, Wanapum*

A few
more passing suns
will see us here no more, and
our dust and bones will mingle
with these same prairies.

I see
as in a vision the
dying spark of our council fires,
the ashes cold and white.

I see
no longer the curling smoke
rising from our lodge poles.

I hear
no longer the songs
of the women
as they prepare the meal.

The antelope have gone;
the buffalo wallows are empty.

Only the wail of the
coyote is heard.

The white man's medicine
is stronger than ours;
his iron horse rushes over
the buffalo trail.

He talks to us
through his 'whispering spirit'
(the telephone).

We are like birds with
a broken wing.
My heart is cold within me.
My eyes are growing dim —

I am old....

— Chief Plenty-Coups, Crow

A single twig breaks,
but the bundle of
twigs is strong.
Someday I
will embrace
our brother
tribes and
draw them
into a bundle
and together we
will win our country
back from the whites.

— *Tecumseh, Shawnee*

We respected our old people
above all others in the tribe.

To live to be so old
they must have been brave
and strong,
and good fighters,
and we aspired to be like them.

We never allowed our old people
to want for anything...

We looked upon our old people
as demigods of a kind,
and we loved them deeply.
They were all our fathers.

65   *— Buffalo Child Long Lance, Sioux*

There was a time when our
people covered the land as the
waves of a wind-ruffled sea
cover its shell-paved floor.
But that time long since
passed... Our people are
ebbing away like a
rapidly receding
tide that will
never return...

Tribe follows tribe, and nation
follows nation, like the waves of
the sea. It is the order of nature,
and regret is useless.

Your time of decay may be distant
but it will certainly come for
even the White Man, whose
God walked and talked
with him as friend
with friend, cannot be
exempt from the
common destiny.

We may be brothers after all.
We will see...

Even the rocks which seem to be
dumb and dead as they swelter
in the sun along the silent
shore thrill with memories
of stirring events connected with the lives of my
people, and the very
dust upon which
you now stand

responds more lovingly to their
footsteps than to yours because it
is rich with the dust of our
ancestors, and our bare feet are
conscious of the sympathetic
touch...

And when the last Red Man shall
have perished and the memory
of my tribe shall have become a myth among the
white man these shores
will swarm with the
invisible dead of
my tribe,

and when your children's
children think themselves
alone in the fields,
the store,
the shop,
upon the highway
or in the silence of the
pathless woods, they will not
be alone...

At night when the streets of your
villages and cities are silent and
you think them deserted they
will throng with the returning
hosts that once filled them and
still love this beautiful land.

The White Man
will never be alone.
Let him be just and
deal kindly with my people
for the dead are not powerless.

Death — I say?
There is no death.
Only a change of worlds.

— *Chief Seattle, Duwamish*

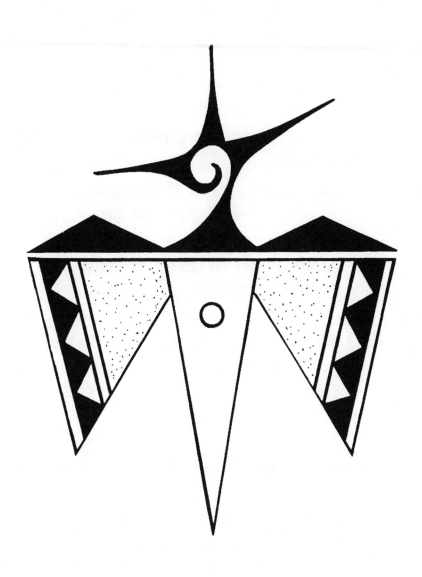

Mother Corn
has fed you, as she has fed
all Hopi people,
since long, long ago
when she was no larger
than my thumb.

Mother Corn
is a promise of food and life.
I grind with gratitude
for the richness of
our harvest,
not with cross feelings
of working too hard.

As I kneel at my grinding stone,
I bow my head in prayer,
thanking the great forces
for provision.

I have received much.

I am willing to
give much in return...
there must be a giving back
for what one receives.

— *Sevenka Qoyawayma, Hopi*

Old age
was simply
a delightful time,
when the old people sat
playing in the sun
with the children
until they
fell asleep.

At last, they failed to wake up.

68   — *Jaytiamo, Acoma*

Oh the comfort,
the inexpressible comfort
of feeling safe with a person,
having neither to
weigh thought
nor
measure words,

but
pouring them all right out,
just as they are,
chaff and grain together,
certain that
a faithful hand
will take and
sift them,
keep
what is worth keeping,
and with a breath of kindness,
blow the rest away.

69   — *anonymous, Shoshone*

May serenity circle
on silent wings
and catch
the whisper of the wind.

70   — *Cheewa James, Modoc*

Cheewa James

In the spring of 1873 a tiny spark of life flickered into existence. The boy was born in a lava cave in northern California as the Modoc Indian War raged around him.

This child, son of Modoc warrior Ski-et-teteko — better known in the white world as Shacknasty Jim — was to be one of the youngest exiles sent to Oklahoma Indian Territory in the fall of 1873 as a prisoner of war. The child would be known as Clark James, father of Clyde James, grandfather of Cheewa.

Cheewa James' Modoc blood is mixed with German and Irish. Born at the Klamath Indian Agency, Oregon, she was raised in Taos, New Mexico. She is enrolled with the Modoc Tribe of Oklahoma.

Cheewa is a veteran television reporter, anchor and producer, winner of the National Golden Mike Award and five UPI awards for reporting and feature documentaries. An accomplished author, she has published over 100 magazine and newspaper articles.

She is a seasoned professional speaker, using Native American principles and thoughts to highlight communication skills and personal development. Cheewa studies and sings American Indian music.

David and Jean Villaseñor

David Villaseñor was born in Mexico of Huichol/Otomi Indian and Spanish descent. After a move to the United States at the age of 16, David lived near and with Indians of the Southwest. It was here that his great love of the Navajo sand paintings developed.

The paintings, he felt, were "one of the most beautiful and hallowed rites of the Navajo, through which his reverence for all creation is made visual, with superb dignity..." The sand paintings are considered to be sacred and are begun, completed, used and destroyed within a 12-hour period.

The illustrations in **Catch the Whisper of the Wind** are adaptations not only from David's beloved sand paintings but from American Indian pottery, basketry and ceremonials from the Southwest.

David is known not only for his "sandscapes" but for his elegant carvings and sculpture. His work can be seen in the Los Angeles County Museum of Natural History and La Plaza de la Raza in Lincoln Park, East Los Angeles.

His wife, the former Jean Gimlin, a gifted artist in her own right, shared a life with David filled with artistic and literary accomplishments. They co-authored several books about sand painting and Indian symbolism. Jean lives in Regina, New Mexico.

Illustrations

Illustrations in book, correlated by number to text

1 - *Pueblo Buffalo*
2 - *Acoma Pueblo Bird*
6 & 10 - *Pueblo Sun Symbols* - The sun is the emissary
 of the Great Spirit, without which all life on Earth
 would perish.
11 - *Pueblo Eagle* - The eagle is a lofty concept,
 denoting inspiration, ideals and courage.
14 - *Santa Domingo Pueblo*
16 - *Isleta Pueblo Rain Bird*
17 - *Pueblo pottery of the Rio Grande* - symbolic of
 the paradoxical world in which we live
19 - *Hohokam Bird* - ancient
20 - *Acoma Pueblo design*
24 - *Pueblo Owl Design*
28 - *Pueblo Grasshopper*
30 - *Apache Ceremonial Figure*
31 - *Zia Pueblo Dragonfly* - the spirit of growth
 Miembres Catfish - ancient pottery design
34 - *Pueblo Cricket Design* - ancient
37 - *Hopi Rain Bird Spirit* - A vortex of energy: the
 spirit of creation is incorporated in all the
 elements which bring forth life.
45 - *Pueblo Bear* - powerful symbol of strength
51 - *Pueblo Turtle Design*
57 - *Acoma Pueblo Water Bird*
61 - *Isleta Pueblo Fish*
62 - *Papago Indian Design*
63 - HORIZON 2000 logo (publisher of — *Catch the
 Whisper of the Wind* —)
 Hohokam Load Carrier - ancient 1000-1200 A.D.
66 - *Zia Pueblo Dragonfly* - the spirit of growth
69 - *Miembres Deer* - ancient design
70 - *Hopi Rain Bird Spirit* - bringing abundance to the
 earth
Illustration page - *Hohokam Flute Player* - joy bringer

Narration

The cassette tape available to compliment this book has selected writings narrated by Cheewa James. The selections are framed in traditional Native American melodies, accented with innovative new sounds from composer George Tricomi.

Narration number from the book and corresponding first line:

1 - What is life?
2 - My heart is filled with joy
3 - We are part fire, and part dream
6 - Everything the power of the world does
8 - Wars are fought to see
10 - The Earth does not belong to man (last part)
12 - Did you know that trees talk
14 - At the edge of the cornfield
17 - A nation is not conquered
18 - When you get married
19 - It is not only now
20 - Marriage among my people
21 - I never did get a woman
22 - It is well to be good
23 - Love songs
25 - Training began with children
26 - If you do bad things
27 - Good acts done
28 - Do not speak of evil
29 - Lose your temper with a child
33 - We who are clay
34 - He who is present
35 - Even if the heavens
37 - He (Ishi) looked upon us

38 - Every struggle
39 - I will not lie to you
41 - In you as in all men
45 - The Indian believes
47 - Have patience
48 - The longer a problem
49 - The selfish man is lonely
50 - Free yourself
51 - A brave man dies
52 - One has to face fear
53 - Do not judge
54 - Kindness
55 - Lose your temper
56 - To be lazy
57 - Do not stop watering the corn
58 - The Ute who follows two rabbits
59 - Honor age
60 - No one likes to be criticized
62 - We live, we die
63 - A few more passing suns
64 - A single twig breaks
65 - We respected our old people
66 - There was a time when
67 - Mother corn
70 - May serenity circle

To order tape call: (916) 369-6616

HORIZON 2000 PRODUCT ORDER FORM

Please send the following items:

Catch the Whisper of the Wind
                                            book $11.95 _____
Catch the Whisper of the Wind
                                    book & cassette $21.95 _____

Write to Publish the Million Dollar Way
by Bud Gardner — 6 audio cassette album —
Must-know principles to sell what you write
                                                    $59.95 _____

Plus shipping and handling - first item $ 3.00 _____

Plus additional postage - each $ 2.00 _____

California residents sales tax at   7.75% _____

                        Total   _____

_____ check enclosed
_____ Mastercard _____ Visa

Card # _____ Exp. date _____

Name on card (please print) _____

Signature and date _____

Name _____

Address _____

City _____ State _____ Zip _____

Phone (___) _____

Call: 1-800-875-1992

HORIZON 2000
2222 Watt Ave., #B12 • Sacramento, CA 95825
(916) 369-6616 • FAX (916) 369-6616
Call for speaking engagements